The New Soccer Coach

Adaptation from the animated series: Anne Paradis
Illustrations taken from the animated series and adapted by Mario Allard

chouette

"Good shot, Caillou!"

Caillou was kicking the ball before soccer practice with his biggest fan, Grandpa.

"I used to play soccer when I was your age," Grandpa said. "Once I even had to use my noggin to score a goal!"

Caillou liked it when Grandpa shared soccer stories.

Grandpa placed two chairs to use as goalposts.
"Let's see if you can score on your old grandpa."
Caillou gave the ball a mighty kick. Grandpa tried
to block the ball, but it bounced into the net.
"Goaaal!" they both shouted.

Grandpa gave Caillou his special high five.
"You two better get going or you'll be late for practice,"
Mommy suggested.
"I hope my new coach is as much fun as you are,
Grandpa!" Caillou said.

When they got to the soccer field, Caillou ran to join his teammates.

"Hi, everyone! Where's our new coach?"

"I don't know, but I hope he's fun," Clementine said.

Someone blew a whistle, and they all turned around.

"Hi team, meet your new coach!"

Caillou was surprised that Grandpa was his new coach.
It made him feel special.
The team gathered around the coach. "I used to play soccer when I was your age," Grandpa began.
Caillou thought Grandpa's soccer stories were just for him. Suddenly, he didn't feel so special anymore.

"Everyone grab a ball and show me how you dribble," said the coach.

Caillou wanted Grandpa to see what a good soccer player he was. He controlled the ball around the cones and ran back as fast as he could.

"Way to go, Caillou!" Grandpa gave Caillou their special high five. Caillou beamed.

Then it was Clementine's turn. Grandpa greeted her with a high five. "Way to go, champ!"
Caillou was startled. Grandpa was using their special high five with everyone.
"Your grandpa is really cool," Clementine said.
Caillou wasn't so sure he liked having Grandpa as his coach.

The next day was Caillou's first game. Coach Grandpa gave instructions to the players. "Caillou and Jason, you'll play defense and protect the goalie."
"But Grandpa, I want to score goals, just like when we play together," Caillou protested.
"Be patient, Caillou. Everyone will get a chance."

Early in the game, the ball shot past Leo, who was playing goalie.
"Don't worry, team! Get back out there and have fun," called Grandpa.

The referee blew the whistle, and the game resumed.
The ball came toward Caillou. He saw his big chance
to score a goal.
"You can do it, Caillou!" Grandpa shouted.

Caillou kicked the ball so hard that his shoe flew off and went into the net. The ball just rolled right past the net. Caillou was upset. He walked over to the bench. Coach Grandpa called a time-out.

"What's the matter, champ?" Grandpa asked.

"I'm no good at soccer," Caillou said.

"And you share our special stories with everyone," Caillou added sheepishly.

Grandpa sighed. "When I'm coach, I have to treat everyone the same way."

Grandpa pulled a medal from his pocket. "I won this soccer medal when I was your age. Keep it to remember that Grandpa is always proud of you, even when I'm your coach."

Caillou hugged Grandpa. "I'm glad you're my coach.
And I'm glad you're my grandpa!"
Caillou leaped back into the game.
He now understood that Grandpa could be his coach,
his grandfather and also one of his biggest fans!

Text: adaptation by Anne Paradis of the animated series CAILLOU,
produced by DHX Media Inc.
All rights reserved.
Original script written by Shelley Hoffman and Robert Pincombe.
Original episode #507B Coach Grandpa
Illustrations: Mario Allard, based on the animated series CAILLOU
Coloration: Eric Lehouillier

The PBS KIDS logo is a registered mark of PBS and is used with permission.

Chouette Publishing would like to thank the Government of Canada and SODEC
for their financial support.

Books
Tax Credit

Gestion
SODEC

Bibliothèque et Archives nationales du Québec and Library and Archives
Canada cataloguing in publication

Paradis, Anne, 1972-
Caillou: the new soccer coach
New edition.

(Playtime)
For children aged 3 and up.

ISBN 978-2-89718-361-5

I. Allard, Mario, 1969-   . II. Title. III. Title: New soccer coach. IV. Series:
Playtime (Montréal, Québec).

PS8631.A713C333 2017   jC813'.6   C2016-941546-5
PS9631.A713C333 2017

Printed in China
10 9 8 7 6 5 4 3 2 1 CHO1985 OCT2016

MEMORY GAME

Goal: Find two identical images among all the pictures in order to form pairs.

How to play: Carefully separate the 32 cards along the dotted line. Shuffle the cards and lay them in rows, face down.

The youngest player goes first. Turn over two cards. If they match, keep the pair and play again. If the cards are different, turn them back over for the next player.

The player who collects the most pairs wins.